THE STORY OF
A CALICO CLOWN

LAURA LEE HOPE

The Story Of A Calico Clown

CHAPTER I

THE GIANT'S SWING

"To-night we shall have a most wonderful time," said the Elephant from the Noah's Ark to a Double Humped Camel who lived in the stall next to him.

"What kind of a time?" asked the Camel. He stood on the toy counter of a big department store, looking across the top of a drum toward a Jack in the Box who was swaying to and fro on his long spring. "What do you call a wonderful time, Mr. Elephant?"

"Oh, having fun," replied the big toy animal, slowly swinging his trunk to and fro. "And to-night the Calico Clown is going to give a special exhibition."

"Oh, is he?" suddenly asked a funny little Wooden Donkey with a head that wagged up and down. "Is he going to climb a string again and burn his red and yellow trousers as he once did?"

"Indeed I am not!" exclaimed the Calico Clown himself. The Clown was leaning against his friend Mr. Jumping Jack, who was a cousin of Jack in the Box. "I'm not going to give any special exhibition like that," went on the Clown. "I'm just going to do a few funny tricks, such as standing on my head and banging my cymbals together. And, I am not sure, but I may ask a riddle."

"Will it be that one about what makes more noise than a pig under a gate?" inquired a Celluloid Doll. "Well, yes, it will be that riddle," replied the Clown, trying to look very stern.

"That's the only riddle he knows," whispered the Elephant.

"What I should like to know," said the Camel, "is why a pig should want to get under a gate, anyhow. Why didn't he stay in his pen?"

"Oh, there's no use trying to make you understand," sighed the Clown. "I'll just have to dance around, do a few jigs, bang my cymbals together, and do things like that to amuse you."

"Well, we'll have a good time to-night, anyhow," said the Celluloid

Doll. "We really haven't had much fun since the Candy Rabbit and the

Monkey on a Stick went away. I wish—"

"Hush!" suddenly called the Calico Clown. "Here come the clerks. The store will soon be filled with customers."

The toys became very still and quiet. This talk among them had taken place in the early morning hours, after a night of jolly good times. But when daylight came, and when clerks and customers filled the store, the toys were no longer allowed to do as they pleased. They could not move about or talk as they could on other occasions.

The Calico Clown was a jolly chap, and he seemed to stand out among all the other toys on the counter. He wore calico trousers of which one leg was red and the other yellow. He had a calico shirt that was spotted, speckled and striped in gay colors, and on each of his hands was a round piece of brass. These pieces of brass were called "cymbals," and the Calico Clown could bang them together as the drummer bangs his cymbals in the band.

I say the Calico Clown could bang his cymbals together, and by that I mean he could do it when no boys or girls or grown folk were looking at him. This was the rule for all the toys. They could move about and talk only when no human eyes were looking. As soon as you glanced at them they became as still and as quiet as potatoes.

But any one who picked up the Calico Clown could make him bang his cymbals together by pressing on his chest. There was a little spring, and also a sort of squeaker, such as you have heard in toy bears or sheep.

Besides being able to clap his cymbals together, the Calico Clown could also move his arms and legs when you pulled certain strings, like those on some Jumping Jacks. The Calico Clown was a lively fellow, as well as being very gaily dressed.

But now all the toys were still and quiet. They sat or stood or were lying down on the counter, waiting for what would happen next. And what generally did happen was that some customers came to the store and bought them.

Already a number of the toys had been sold and taken away. There was the Sawdust Doll. She was the first to go. Then the White Rocking Horse had been bought for a boy named Dick, a brother of Dorothy, who now owned the Sawdust Doll. The Lamb on Wheels had been purchased by a jolly sailor, and when the Lamb saw him she feared she would be taken on an ocean trip and made seasick. But the sailor gave the Lamb to a little girl named Mirabell. And, in the course of time, her brother Arnold was given a Bold Tin Soldier and some soldier men.

The Candy Rabbit—about whom I have told you in a book, as I have told you of these other toys—the Candy Rabbit was given as an Easter present to a little girl named Madeline, and her brother Herbert had, later, been given the Monkey on a Stick.

The Calico Clown was looking over at the Celluloid Doll, thinking how pretty she was, and he was also thinking of the Sawdust Doll, whom he had liked very much, when, all of a sudden, it seemed as if a whirlwind had blown into the toy department.

A boy with a very loud voice and feet that tramped and stamped on the floor rushed up to the counter.

"I want a toy! I want something to play with!" cried this boy. "I want a Jumping Jack and I want a Noah's Ark! You said you'd get me something if I let the dentist pull that tooth, and now you've got to! I want a lot of toys!" he cried to the lady who was with him.

"Yes, Archibald. But please be quiet!" begged his mother. "I will get you a toy. Which one do you want?"

"I want this Elephant!" cried the boy who, I am afraid, was rather rude. He caught the Elephant up by his trunk, and twisted the poor animal around.

"Goodness me, sakes alive! I'm getting dizzy," thought the Elephant.

"I hope this boy is not to be my master!"

And this, it would seem, was not going to happen. Suddenly the boy dropped the Elephant.

"I don't want this toy! He can't do anything!" the boy shouted. "I want something that jiggles and joggles and does things! Oh, I want this one!" and, as true as I'm telling you, that boy caught up the Calico Clown.

"Well, I guess this is the last of me!" thought the Calico Clown. "I will not last very long in the hands of this rude chap."

The boy had grabbed up the Calico Clown and had thrown the Elephant down so hard that the Celluloid Doll was knocked over.

"Be careful, little boy, if you please," gently said the girl clerk.

"Oh, I've got to have this Clown!" went on the rude boy. "I don't care for other toys. Does this fellow do anything?" he asked of the clerk, while his mother looked on, hardly knowing what to say. Archibald had just been to the dentist's to have a tooth pulled, so perhaps we should forgive him for being a little rough.

"The Clown plays his cymbals when you touch him here," and the clerk pointed to the spring hidden in the chest of the gay fellow, under his speckled, striped and spotted calico jacket.

"Oh, I'll touch him all right! I'll punch him!" cried the boy, and he jabbed the Calico Clown so hard in the chest that the cymbals rattled together like marbles in a boy's pocket.

"He's dandy! I want him!" cried the boy. "What else does he do?" he asked.

"He moves his arms and legs when you pull these strings," was the answer, and the clerk showed the boy how to do it.

"Oh, he's a jolly toy!" cried Archibald. "I'll have some fun with him when I show him to the other fellows. Hi! Look at him jig!" and he pulled the strings so fast that it seemed as if the poor Clown would turn somersaults.

"I can see what will happen to me," thought the Clown. "I shall come to pieces in about a week, and be thrown in the ash can. Why can't he be nice and quiet?"

But Archibald was not that kind of boy. He seemed to want to make a noise or do something all the while. Most of his toys at home were broken, and that is why his mother had to promise to get him another before he would let her take him to the dentist's to have an aching tooth pulled.

"I want this Clown!" cried Archibald, making the cymbals bang together again and again.

"Very well, you may have it," his mother replied.

"I'll wrap it up for you," said the clerk, and the poor Clown was quickly smothered in a wrapping of paper around which a string was tied.

"Here is your toy, Archibald," said his mother, when the plaything came back ready to be taken out of the store. The mother had taken it from the clerk, and now she handed it to her little boy.

And so he carried the Calico Clown away, without giving the poor, jolly fellow a chance to say good-bye to the Elephant, the Camel or the Celluloid Doll.

"Now our good time for to-night is spoiled," sadly thought the

Elephant. "Our jolly comrade is gone!"

All the way home in the automobile Archibald kept punching the red and yellow Clown in the chest and banging the cymbals together until the boy's mother said:

"Oh, Archibald, please be quiet! My head aches!"

"All right, I'll make my Clown jiggle!" said the boy, who really loved his mother, though sometimes he was rude.

Then he pulled the strings until the poor Clown thought his arms and legs would come off, so fast were they jerked about.

When Archibald reached home with his new toy he ran out into the street to find some of his playmates. He saw a boy named Pete and another named Sam.

"Look what I've got!" cried Archibald.

"A Jumping Jack!" exclaimed Sam.

"It's a Calico Clown, and he can do everything," said Archibald. "He's like one in a circus, and he can do funny tricks. He can jiggle his arms and legs and play the cymbals. I'll show you!"

He worked the Clown so fast that the red and yellow chap grew dizzy again.

"That's fine!" said Sam. "I wish I had a Clown like that."

"Can he do the giant's swing?" asked Pete.

"What's the giant's swing?" Archibald wanted to know.

"It's something the men do in a circus," was the answer. "Here, I have some string in my pocket. We'll make a trapeze in your back yard and we'll have the Calico Clown do the giant's swing."

"Oh, that'll be fun!" cried Archibald.

"Yes, it may be fun for you," thought the Calico Clown, "but what about me? What is the giant's swing, anyhow? Oh, I wish I were back on the toy counter!"

CHAPTER II

A BROKEN LEG

Sam and Pete hurried with Archibald to his back yard. Archibald carried the red and yellow Calico Clown in his hands. Now and then the boy would punch the gay fellow in the chest, making the cymbals clang together with a bang. Again Archibald would pull the strings, causing the Calico Clown to jiggle his arms and legs.

"You're a nice toy, all right," said Archibald. "I like my Clown!"

"But wait until I make him do the giant's swing!" exclaimed Pete.

"That will be worth seeing!"

When the boys reached a tree in Archibald's yard, Pete found a piece of broken broom handle for the bar of the trapeze. From his pocket he took some strong pieces of string. With these the broomstick was tied to the limb of a tree, so that it hung down and swung to and fro like a swing.

"Now well put the Clown on," Pete called to Archibald, when the trapeze was finished.

"How are you going to make him stay on?" asked Sam.

"Oh, I can tie him on with another piece of string," Pete answered.

"That's easy!" yelled Archibald.

It did not take Pete long to tie the Calico Clown on the swinging trapeze. It was quite high from the ground, and as the little toy man looked down and saw how far below him the green grass was, his knees seemed to shake and his cymbals to tremble.

"Oh, if I should fall now I would be broken to pieces!" said the Calico Clown to himself, for of course he dared not speak aloud now, and he dared not move by himself. "This is much higher than when I climbed the string in the toy store and caught fire at the gas jet. This is much higher than I ever was up before," sighed the Clown.

"Is he ready to do the giant's swing now?" asked Sam.

"In a minute," answered Pete.

Once the Clown was tied on, Pete began to swing the trapeze to and fro. Farther and farther swung the Calico Clown, and, as he moved to and fro, his cymbals clanged together. His arms and legs also jiggled and jumped, as they had done when Archibald pulled the strings.

Pete stood behind the trapeze and gave it little pushes with his hands every now and then. This made it swing farther and farther.

"Oh, it almost turned all the way over!" suddenly cried Archibald.

"That's what I want it to do," said Pete. "When the trapeze goes all the way over and around and around, that's the giant's swing I was telling you about. Watch!"

Archibald and Sam watched, and in another moment the trapeze swung up and over so hard that it turned around and around in a regular circle.

"Hurray! There she goes!" cried Pete.

"Oh, look!" exclaimed Sam.

"Say, that's great!" yelled Archibald. "I didn't know my Calico Clown could do that!"

As for the Calico Clown himself, he did not know it either, and he felt very bad that he was made to do the giant's swing.

"Oh, how dizzy it makes me feel!" he said to himself. "I know I'm going to fall!"

He could feel the strings that tied him to the broomstick bar beginning to loosen. The Calico Clown shut his eyes, thinking that if he did not see the green grass whirling around beneath him he would not feel so dizzy. Around and around he went in the giant's swing.

And then, all of a sudden, something broke. It was the string holding the Calico Clown to the broomstick. And when the string broke off flew the Clown!

He flew off just when the trapeze was at the highest point, and away through the air sailed the red and yellow toy, as if he had been shot from a cannon.

"Oh, look at that!" cried Archibald, "Now you've gone and done it,

Pete!"

"He busted loose!" shouted Sam.

"If he falls and breaks, you've got to get me another," cried

Archibald.

"I'm going to fall, all right," thought the poor Clown to himself, "and I shouldn't be a bit surprised if I broke into bits!"

One can not go sailing through the air forever, even if one is a Calico Clown. And, after being flung off the trapeze and shooting along high above the green grass, the Calico Clown felt himself falling down.

Once more he shut his eyes, as he could do this without the boys seeing him. His arms and legs jiggled and joggled about, and his cymbals clanged with a tinkling sound.

"Oh, dear!" sighed the Calico Clown.

There came a soft, dull thud on the grass. That was the Calico Clown falling down. He felt a sudden, sharp pain go through him, and then he seemed to faint away.

For a time the Calico Clown knew nothing of what happened. Archibald, Sam and Pete ran over to where the toy had fallen. Archibald was the first to pick it up. The cymbals were still fast to the Clown's hands, and so were the jiggling strings attached to his arms and legs. But something was wrong.

"Oh, one of his legs is broken!" cried Archibald. "My Calico Clown is spoiled! Pete, you've broken one of his legs!"

And that was what had happened. In his fall from the trapeze the poor red and yellow toy had cracked one of his wooden legs. It was the one on which he wore the red half of his trousers.

"I—I didn't mean to do that," said Pete.

"Well, you did it; and now you have to get me another toy!" exclaimed

Archibald. "If you don't I'll tell my mother on you."

"Oh, Arch!" exclaimed Sam.

"Oh, all right. I'll get you another," said Pete quickly. "You can come over to my house now, and I'll give you anything I have in place of your Calico Clown. I didn't think his leg would break so easily."

The three boys, with Archibald carrying the poor, broken-legged Clown, hurried out of the yard. As they were going to Pete's house they met a boy named Sidney, who was a brother of Herbert and Madeline. Madeline owned the Candy Rabbit, and Herbert had a Monkey on a Stick—both of them toys that had once lived in the same store with the Calico Clown.

"What have you?" asked Sidney of Archibald.

"A Calico Clown," was the answer. "He was new a little while ago, but Pete put him on a trapeze and made him do the giant's swing and now he's done for—he's got a broken leg."

"What are you going to do with him?" asked Sidney.

"He's going to make me give him one of my toys in place of the Clown," answered Pete. "Of course it was my fault he broke—I guess I didn't tie him on tight enough. And I'm willing to give Archie another toy for him, but—"

Sidney suddenly thrust his hand into his pocket and pulled out a gaily painted top that hummed and made music when you spun it.

"I'll trade you that for your Calico Clown," said Sidney to Archibald.

"But the Clown has a broken leg," explained Pete.

"I don't care. Maybe I can mend it," Sidney answered. "Once I fixed a

Jumping Jack that had lost his head."

"Well, if you did that, you can fix a Clown that has only a broken leg," said Sam. "Go on and trade with him, Archie."

"All right, I will," decided Archibald. He held out the broken Clown and in trade took the musical top.

"Now I don't have to give you any of my toys, do I, Archie?" asked

Pete.

"Nope," Archibald answered. "I'd rather have this top than a broken

Calico Clown."

While he was being traded for the top the Calico Clown came out of his faint. His broken leg did not hurt so much now. He felt more like himself.

"Oh, ho!" he thought. "I am to have a new master, it seems. Well, I hope it will not be one who makes me do the giant's swing. Once is enough for that!"

Archibald went off with Sam and Pete to try the musical top. Sidney carried the Calico Clown toward the house where Madeline and Herbert lived.

"I'll fix you as good as new," said Sidney, looking at the dangling, broken leg.

And, as Sidney walked along, all of a sudden he heard his sister calling.

"Oh, quick, somebody! Somebody come quick! He's fallen into the water!"

CHAPTER III

THE CLOWN'S DANCE

Sidney stuffed the Calico Clown into his pocket and ran as fast as he could toward his sister. He saw her standing near a little fountain in the side yard of their home.

"What's the matter, Madeline?" asked Sidney, making sure the Calico

Clown was not falling out of his pocket as he ran along.

"Oh, he's in the water!" said the little girl.

"Who is?" her brother wanted to know. "Who's in?"

"My Candy Rabbit. I set him on the edge of the fountain so he could watch the birds having a bath, and he fell right in."

Sidney looked toward the fountain. He saw nothing of the Candy Rabbit.

"You can't see him 'cause he's over the edge, down inside," went on Madeline. "I can't reach and get him, or I'd fish him out myself. And if he stays there very long he'll melt, as he almost did once when he fell into the bathtub. Oh, please get him out for me."

"I will!" promised Sidney.

"Oh, is it possible I am to see my dear old friend, the Candy Rabbit, again?" thought the Calico Clown, who, though stuffed into Sidney's pocket, had heard all that was said. The toys could hear and understand talk at all times, except when they were asleep. The broken leg of the gay red and yellow chap did not hurt him very much just now. "I shall certainly be glad to see the Candy Rabbit again," the Clown thought. "And Sidney had better hurry and get him out of the water, or he surely will melt, and that would be dreadful."

The fountain in the yard of the house where Herbert, Madeline and Sidney lived was rather a high one. The little girl could just reach up to the rim of the basin to set her Rabbit there, but, once he had toppled over and was down inside, she could neither see nor reach him.

"You'll have to stand on something or you can't get him," Madeline said to Sidney. "Shall I get you a box?"

"No, I'll stand on my tiptoes," he answered. And he did, thus making himself tall enough to reach over into the water and fish out the Candy Rabbit.

Out that sweet fellow came, dripping wet, but not much harmed.

"Oh, he didn't melt, did he?" asked Madeline. "I'm so glad!"

"He hasn't melted yet," answered Sidney, as he handed the Easter toy to his sister. "But you'd better put him in the sun to dry, or he may crumble away."

"I will," Madeline promised.

As Sidney turned to walk away, the Calico Clown fell out of his pocket.

"What's that? Where'd you get him?" cried Madeline. At the same time the Candy Rabbit saw the gay red and yellow chap from the toy store.

"Oh, there's my dear old Clown friend!" thought the Rabbit, all wet as he was. "How in the wide world did he get here?"

But of course he could not ask, any more than the Calico Clown could answer.

And when the Clown, lying on the grass where he had fallen from

Sidney's pocket, saw the Candy Rabbit, the Clown said to himself:

"Yes, there he is! The same one I knew before. Oh, if we could only get together by ourselves and talk! How much we could say!"

Sidney picked the Calico Clown up off the grass.

"Where did you get him?" asked Madeline again. "He's awfully cute. I saw one like that in the store where Aunt Emma got my Candy Rabbit."

"Maybe this is the same one," Sidney answered. "I traded off my musical top to Archibald for the Clown. His leg is broken."

"Whose—Archibald's?" asked Madeline, in surprise.

"No, the Clown's," answered Sidney, with a laugh. "I'm going to fix it. Course a Calico Clown is worth more than a musical top, for the Clown is new and my top was old. But a Clown with a broken leg isn't worth so much."

"Is it worth anything?" asked Madeline. "I mean can you fix him?"

"Oh, yes," her brother answered. "He can still bang his cymbals, and he can jiggle both his arms and the leg that isn't broken."

Sidney punched the Clown in the chest, and the red and yellow fellow clapped his hands together and made the cymbals tinkle. Then Sidney pulled the strings and the two arms of the Clown went up and down, and one leg kicked out as nicely as you please. But the other leg did not move.

"That's the leg that's broken," Sidney explained. "He got broken when

Pete made him do the giant's swing."

"He looks as though he was trying to dance on one leg!" laughed

Madeline. "He's awfully cute, but he's funny!"

"I'll soon fix him, and he'll be as good as ever," declared her brother. "You'd better go and put your Rabbit in the sun to dry."

So Madeline did this, and very glad the sweet chap was to feel the warm sun on his back, for he had been made quite drippy and sticky by having fallen into the fountain.

Sidney, as I have told you, was a boy who could mend things. Once he had fixed Herbert's toy boat that was broken, and, another time, he had glued a head back on Madeline's Celluloid Doll.

"And I think I can glue my Clown's broken leg," thought Sidney, as he went toward the kitchen. There, he remembered, the cook always kept a tube of sticky glue.

"What are you going to mend now?" asked the cook.

"A broken leg," Sidney answered.

"Oh, you can't mend a broken leg with glue!" cried the cook. "You had much better call in the doctor. Whose leg is it?"

"I'm going to be the toy doctor," the little boy went on. "It's the wooden leg of a Calico Clown I'm going to mend."

"Oh, that's different," said the cook. "Well, here's the glue."

She handed Sidney the tube. He took it and his Clown over to a table. Pushing up the red trouser Sidney saw where the Clown's leg was broken. The wood was cracked and splintered, but the two pieces were there.

"I'll just glue them together," said the boy. And this he did. Then, as he knew that glue must set, or get hard, he put his Calico Clown away on a shelf in a closet, where the toy chap saw something that made him wonder.

At first, in the darkness, the Clown could not make out what or who it was on the shelf in the closet with him. Then, as his eyes became accustomed to the gloom, he noticed that it was a Cat.

"Oh, are you a toy, too?" asked the Calico Clown politely, for he wanted company and some one to talk to.

"No, I am not exactly a toy," answered the Cat.

"You look like one," the Clown said. "There was one just like you in our store, only that cat's head wobbled."

"Well, my head doesn't wobble—it comes off," said the Cat.

"Your head comes off!" cried the Clown in great surprise. "I should think that would hurt!"

"No, it's made to do that," the Cat explained. "You see I'm a match safe, and I also have a place inside me where burned matches may be put. To put them in me you have to lift off my head. It doesn't hurt at all—I'm used to it."

"Oh, that's different," said the Calico Clown. "Well, I am very glad to meet you. Do you know the Candy Rabbit?"

The Cat said she did, and very well, too.

"He sleeps here on the closet shelf with me every night," she added.

"You'll see him, pretty soon!"

"I shall be very glad to," remarked the Clown. "Excuse me for not sitting up as I talk," he said, for Sidney had laid him down flat on his back. "The truth of the matter," went on the Clown, "is that my leg was broken a while ago, and the boy just glued it together."

"Oh, I'm so sorry!" mewed the Match-Safe Cat.

"I'm not—I'm glad," said the Clown. "If it wasn't glued I'd be a slimpsy lopsy sort of chap."

"Oh, I didn't mean I was sorry your leg was GLUED, I meant that I was sorry it was BROKEN," went on the Cat. "Now let's tell each other our adventures."

So they did, talking until late in the evening when, suddenly, the closet door was opened by Madeline. Of course, then the Cat and the Calico Clown had to be very still and quiet.

"There, I guess you'll be best in the closet for the rest of the night," said Madeline to her Candy Rabbit Easter toy. "You'll be all dry in the morning, I hope," and she thrust the Rabbit back on the shelf and shut the door.

"Oh, my dear Calico Clown friend!" cried the Candy Rabbit, as soon as it was safe for the toys to speak, "how glad I am to see you again."

"And I am glad to see you," said the Clown. "I rather like it here with the Cat."

"But why are you lying flat on your back?" asked the Candy Rabbit. "You used to be such a lively, jolly fellow. Come, get up and give us one of your old-time jigs or dances."

"I'm very sorry, but I can't," answered the Clown. Then he told about his glued, broken leg, and how he would have to lie very stiff and straight and keep quiet.

"But maybe, toward morning, I'll be well again, and then I can dance for you," he promised.

"I hope so," mewed the Cat. "I have never seen a Calico Clown do a dance."

"You should see him—he is quite wonderful," whispered the Candy

Rabbit behind his paw.

"Well, if I can't dance for you, I can ask a riddle," said the Clown, after a bit. "What makes more noise than a pig under—"

"Oh, PLEASE don't start that over again," begged the Candy Rabbit. "You used to ask it in the store, and none of us could think of the answer. Don't tell riddles! Let's just talk!"

So the toys talked together and told one another their different adventures. The night passed. Madeline, Herbert and Sidney slept, and Sidney dreamed of the fun he would have with his Calico Clown when the broken leg was firmly glued together again.

And as the night passed the glue dried and set, and the Clown, feeling his leg growing better, grew happier.

"I say!" he called out just before morning to the Rabbit and the Cat.

"Are you asleep?"

"I was, but I am awake now," the sugar Bunny answered.

"And I am awake too," added the Cat.

"Then I will dance for you," went on the Clown. "My leg is better."

He stood up and he cut such funny antics by clapping his cymbals together, standing first on one leg and then on the other, jiggling his hands and feet, that the Cat went into mews of laughter and the Rabbit chuckled until his pink nose seemed to wrinkle all up like an accordion.

CHAPTER IV

UP IN A TREE

Faster and faster danced the Calico Clown. No one needed to pull his strings now, for he could dance by himself, no eyes of children or grown folk being in the closet to watch him.

Up and down, first to this side and then to the other, now on his left foot and now on his right, tapping his cymbals softly together, and wagging his head, the Calico Clown amused the Match-Safe Cat and the sugar Bunny in the closet.

"Oh, don't dance any more! Please stop!" begged the Candy Rabbit, holding one paw to his side.

"Don't you like it?" asked the Calico Clown, rather surprised.

"Oh, yes!" was the answer. "But your dance is so funny that it makes me laugh so hard that my ears ache! Do please stop!"

"Yes, please do," begged the Cat. "If you don't, I'm afraid I'll laugh so hard my head may come off and roll to the floor."

"Oh, I wouldn't want THAT to happen!" exclaimed the Clown, as he brought his queer, jerky dance to an end. "If you'd rather, I could tell a riddle."

"Not the one about what makes more noise than a pig under a gate!" exclaimed the Candy Rabbit. "Don't ask that one!"

"Well, it's the only one I know," said the Clown. "I'll try to think of another. But, anyhow, I'll stop my dancing. However, I'm glad for one reason that I did it. It shows that my broken leg is almost as good as the other. A bit stiff, perhaps, but almost as good."

"Yes, you danced as well as I ever saw you jig back in the toy store," said the Rabbit. "You have made the night pass very pleasantly for us."

"You have indeed," added the Cat. "We appreciate your dancing and your fun very much."

"Thank you, both," replied the Calico Clown. "It is a pleasure to do things for fellows such as you."

Then they rested quietly.

A little later Sidney opened the door of the closet to see if his Calico Clown was all right. There lay the yellow and red chap on his back, with one leg stuck straight up in the air, as if he had just kicked a football and then had fallen down.

"Why! Why!" exclaimed Sidney in surprise. "I didn't leave my Clown like THAT!"

"What has happened to him?" asked Madeline, who came to see if her

Candy Rabbit was dry.

"He has one leg stuck up in the air," went on her brother. "I left him lying flat on his back, so the broken leg I mended would get good and hard and stiff again. Now look at him!"

"It IS funny," agreed Madeline. "Didn't you move him?"

"I didn't touch him, and I don't believe anybody has come to this closet since I put him here, except you. Wouldn't it be funny, Madeline, if the Clown got up by himself to see if he could walk on his glued leg?"

"Yes, it would be very funny," agreed the little girl. "But maybe my

Rabbit helped him, or this Match-Safe Cat. Maybe they moved the

Clown!"

"How could they?" Sidney wanted to know.

"They couldn't, unless they came to life," went on Madeline in a whisper. "And sometimes," she went on, looking around to make sure no one else heard her, "sometimes I think that our toys CAN do things by themselves when we can't see them."

"Oh, ho! Course they can't do anything!" laughed Sidney.

But if he could have seen the Calico Clown dancing on the closet shelf, and if he could have heard the Cat and the Candy Rabbit laughing until one's head nearly came off and the other had pains in his ears, then Sidney would have thought differently, wouldn't he?

"Well, anyhow, I'm going to take my Calico Clown out and see how he jumps around this morning," said Sidney, after a while.

Sidney found that the Calico Clown was almost as good an acrobat, or jumper, as ever. When punched in the chest, the Clown would bang his cymbals together. And when the strings were pulled, out shot the arms and legs like those of a Jumping Jack, only in different fashion.

The red and yellow trousers of the Clown had not been soiled by his giant's swing accident, and Sidney had been careful not to get any spots of glue on his toy when he mended him.

"The only thing wrong is that the broken leg is a little stiffer than the other," Sidney said, as he made his Clown do all sorts of funny tricks. "I suppose that leg is a little shorter, or maybe the glue made it stiff. But he is just what I want, and I'd rather have him than the musical top I traded for him. Maybe Herbert and I can get up a little circus, as Herbert once had a show with his Monkey on a Stick. A clown belongs in a circus, and so do monkeys. Maybe we'll have one."

The Calico Clown, who heard Sidney say this, thought it would be very jolly to be in a circus.

Sidney certainly liked the Calico Clown. He made him do many funny tricks for the boys and girls—Dick, Dorothy, Mirabell, Arnold, and for Madeline and Herbert, who were Sidney's brother and sister.

"With my Monkey on a Stick and your Calico Clown we surely can have a fine circus some day," said Herbert, as he and Sidney were playing out on the porch one warm, summer day.

The Monkey and Clown had been glad to see each other when they met again after having been separated at the store. Each one had different adventures to tell.

All of a sudden, as Herbert and Sidney, with their Monkey and Clown toys, were making each other laugh by the funny antics of the two playthings, a voice called:

"Boys, do you want some bread and jam?"

"Oh, I should say we did!" cried Herbert.

"We're coming," answered Sidney, for it was the jolly, good-natured cook who had called to them from her kitchen where she had just made some fresh raspberry jam.

Leaving the Monkey and the Clown on the porch, the boys ran around to the side door for their jam and bread.

"Now we have a chance to talk," said the Monkey to the Clown.

"Yes, but it will not be for very long," was the answer. "Those boys will soon be back here. They'll not eat forever. I was just wondering—"

"What?" asked the Monkey, for the Calico Clown suddenly stopped speaking and looked down the street. "What were you wondering?"

"Well, just NOW I am wondering if that is your brother," went on the Clown, pointing toward the gate with one hand on which was fastened a clanging cymbal. "Look, here comes a chap who looks just like you, except that he has no stick, and his cap is blue, while yours is red. And hark! I hear music!"

"Oh, it's a hand organ, and that's a real, live monkey you see!" exclaimed the Monkey on a Stick. "It is true he looks like me, but we are no relation. He is a live monkey and I am a toy."

"Here he comes now!" cried the Calico Clown, and, as he spoke, the hand-organ man, making music, came along, and the live monkey ran into the yard and up on the steps. And then a dreadful thing happened!

For the live monkey quickly caught up the Calico Clown, and, holding the red and yellow chap in his hands, the long-tailed creature climbed up into a tree. Yes, indeed, as true as I'm telling you, the live monkey carried the Calico Clown up into a tree!

CHAPTER V

TAKEN DOWN TOWN

The Calico Clown was so surprised at the quick action of the monkey in catching him by one leg and carrying him up into the tree, that, for a moment or two, the toy said nothing. But as the hand-organ monkey climbed higher and higher the Clown finally cried:

"Here! Hold on if you please! What are you going to do?"

"Oh, just have some fun!" answered the monkey in a laughing voice. You see, he could understand and speak toy talk, just as the Calico Clown knew how to talk and understand animal language.

[Illustration with caption: Calico Clown Amuses the Monkey.]

"Well, it may be fun for you," went on the Clown, "but I don't like it! This is no fun for me! Ouch! Look out for my leg!" the Clown suddenly cried, as the monkey banged him against a branch of the tree.

"What about your leg?" asked the monkey, sitting down on a branch and winding his tail around it so he wouldn't fall off. "I don't see anything the matter."

"I mean look out and don't hurt my broken leg," went on the Clown. "Sidney, the little boy who owns me, glued it, but if you bang it too hard it may break all over again and then I'll be in a mighty bad fix."

"Oh, excuse me. I'll be careful," said the monkey.

"Well, I wish you'd take me down out of this tree," begged the Calico

Clown. "I don't see why you brought me up here, anyhow."

"Oh, I just grabbed hold of you and brought you up here for fun," said the monkey. "I felt like playing. And I had to do it quickly, or my master would have stopped me. Every time I grab up anything he doesn't want me to take, I have to climb a tree. He can't chase me up there, though he'd like to lots of times, I guess."

"I thought hand-organ monkeys had collars around their necks, and a long rope fast to that which their masters held," said the Clown.

"Well, I had that, too, but I took the rope off a little while ago, so I could run loose," explained the live monkey. "I want to have some fun. Can you do anything to amuse me?" and he looked at the cymbals on the Calico Clown's hands and at the strings which were fast to his legs and arms.

"I can ask you a riddle about what makes more noise than a pig under a gate," said the Clown. "Shall I?"

"Please don't do that," begged the monkey. "I never was any good at guessing riddles. Can't you do anything else?"

"Yes, a few things," the Clown said. Then he banged his cymbals together and began to jiggle his arms and legs in such a funny way that the monkey who was holding him laughed and laughed and laughed.

"Oh, you are too funny for anything!" cried the monkey. "I'm glad I picked you up. Oh, excuse me while I laugh a little harder!"

The monkey set the Clown down astraddle the limb of a tree near the trunk, and quite a distance up from the ground. Then the monkey laughed so hard that, if he had not been holding on by his tail, he surely would have fallen. For the Clown kept on doing his funny antics and tricks, and the monkey kept on laughing until he had to hold his sides with feet and hands, they ached so.

"Oh, I'm so glad I met you!" said the monkey, when he had a chance between his fits of laughter. "I hope my master comes through this street every day with his hand organ. I'll be looking for you."

"And I'll be looking for you—to keep out of your way, if I can," thought the Clown, though he did not say it out loud.

The monkey finally grew a little quiet, and he was just going to ask the Clown to do some more jiggling when, all at once, the music of the hand organ stopped, and the Italian man cried:

"Ah, Jacko! I see you! Up-a in de tree. Bad monk! Come down right away to your Tony! Come, Jacko!"

"Oh, goodness me! I've got to go. My fun is over! Now I've got to go to work gathering pennies in my cap!" said the monkey. "Good-bye!" he called to the Calico Clown, and down out of the tree the monkey began to climb, swinging from limb to limb by his tail, as he used to do in the cocoanut groves of the forest where he had once lived.

"Here! Come back and get me! Don't leave me up in a tree like this!" begged the Calico Clown, who had sat down astride the limb after he had done his last funny trick. "Come and get me!"

"Sorry, but I haven't time! My master is calling me! I must go!" answered the monkey, hurrying more than ever. Down the tree he swung.

"Oh take me down! Don't leave me like this!" begged the Clown. But it was of no use. There he was, left all alone, high up in a tree, sitting on a branch.

Of course neither Tony, the music man, nor Sidney nor Herbert had heard this talk between the toy and the animal, for they spoke in a language that only a few can understand. The organ grinder was anxious for his monkey to come back, and he watched him scrambling down the tree. The two boys, who had gone to get bread and jam, came back to the front yard. They saw the organ grinder and his monkey, and, for the moment, they forgot all about their Clown and the Monkey on a Stick. They did not look toward the porch, or they would have noticed that the Clown was gone, though the toy Monkey was still there. The live monkey was dancing toward the boys, holding out his cap for pennies.

And the Calico Clown was up in the tree, not knowing how in the world he was ever going to get down.

"Oh, look at the monkey!" cried Herbert, as he saw the music man's long-tailed animal.

"He's nice," said Sidney. "He's like your Monkey on a Stick, only bigger, Herb. I'm going in and ask mother for a penny."

"So'm I!" said Herbert.

Still thinking that their own toys were safe on the porch, the little boys ran back into the house, where each one got a penny for the hand-organ monkey. And the monkey took off his blue cap to gather the pennies for his master.

"Good boys!" said the Italian with a smile, and he played another tune for them. And then it was time for him to travel on.

"Come along, Jacko!" he called to his monkey, and then he fastened the rope back on his monkey's collar and made him jump up on the organ. Then the two of them went down the street.

"Oh, there he goes!" thought the poor Calico Clown, still up in the tree. "Oh, he's going to leave me here! Oh, what shall I do?"

Well might he ask that. What could he do? How was he going to get down?

Herbert and Sidney, standing at the gate, saw the music man turn around the corner of the street.

"Now we'll go back and play with my Monkey and your Clown," said

Herbert. "We'll practice for the circus we're going to have."

"That'll be fun!" laughed Sidney.

But when the two boys went back to the porch—well, you know, as well as I, what happened. They saw the Monkey on a Stick, but no Clown!

"Why—why, where is he?" asked Sidney, looking around. "Did you take him, Herb? Did you take my Calico Clown?"

"No, of course not," answered Herbert. "They were both here when we went to get our bread and jam. Oh, Sid! I know what happened!" he suddenly exclaimed.

"What?" asked his brother.

"The hand-organ monkey took your Clown away with him!" went on

Herbert.

At first Sidney thought that this might be so, but, after thinking over the matter for a moment, he shook his head and answered:

"No, the live monkey didn't take my Clown. Don't you remember? He came up here with his cap in his hand to get our pennies. Then, when he went away, he was sitting on top of the organ and he had his cap off and so did the music man, and they didn't either of them have my Clown."

"Yes, I guess that's right," Herbert said. "But he's gone."

"We've got to find my Clown," said Sidney. "I want him back, and we can't have a circus without him. We've GOT to find him."

"Yes, we have," agreed Herbert. "Maybe Carlo, the dog, came and carried him away."

"Maybe," said Sidney. They blamed lots of things on poor Carlo, and sometimes he did do tricks. But this was not one of those times. So the two boys began searching for the Calico Clown.

As for that jolly chap himself he was still up in the tree. And he was not so very jolly just then, either. He did not once think of asking his pig riddle.

"I wonder if I can wiggle down?" he asked himself. "There is no one to see me now, and I can move about. I'm going to try to get down."

He wiggled and he woggled, whatever that is, and managed to get one leg over the limb, so both were on the same side. The Clown was just going to try to swing to the next lowest branch, as he had seen the live monkey do, when, all of a sudden, he slipped and fell.

"Oh, dear! Another accident! This is going to be a bad one—worse than the giant's swing!" he cried.

Down, down, down, he fell. What was going to happen?

Now, just about this time, it chanced that a man was passing under the tree. This man had on a large, loose coat with large pockets on the sides, and he was so used to carrying things in his pockets that each nearly always stood wide open, like a hungry mouth, waiting for some one to fill it.

And, as luck would have it, the man came under the tree just as the Calico Clown slipped and fell. And so, instead of falling to the ground, the Clown fell into one of the wide open side pockets of the man's coat. And the man never knew about it—at least for a time.

"Oh, my goodness me, what a narrow escape!" exclaimed the Clown as he landed safely in the soft pocket. "This is better than falling on the hard ground. But I wonder what will happen to me now."

And well might he ask that, for the man, not knowing the Clown was in his pocket, hurried on down town to his office.

CHAPTER VI

IN THE OFFICE

The Man, into whose pocket the Calico Clown had fallen from the tree, hurried along the street, not knowing a thing of what had happened. He was anxious to get to his office to look after his business, for he was a very busy Man. He kept other folks busy, too—clerks and office boy and a girl to write letters on the typewriter.

Now, as it happened, the Man was a little late that morning, and when he reached his office he was in such haste that he did not take time to do anything before he sat down in his big chair to look over his mail.

"Please write some letters for me on the typewriter," he said to Miss

Jones, who worked the machine.

Miss Jones sat down and became very busy. The Man told her what to write and she banged away on the machine. Every once in a while she would look at the Man when he paused to think of something else to say. And once, as she did this, a queer look came over the face of Miss Jones. Then she smiled and next she burst right out into a loud laugh.

And the funny part of it was that just then the Man was telling her to put in a letter something like this:

"I am very, very sorry to tell you that I can not do as you want me to."

And, just as he said the word "sorry," Miss Jones laughed her very hardest.

"Eh! What's the matter? What is so very funny about my saying I am sorry?" asked the Man. The girl typewriter and the office boy called him "the Boss" behind his back, and they liked him very much, for he was kind and good to them.

"Oh, dear! I MUST laugh!" said Miss Jones.

Miss Jones pointed to something sticking out of his side coat pocket.

The Man put his hand there and pulled out—the Calico Clown!

You should have seen the strange look come over the Man's face. Then he laughed as hard as Miss Jones, and the office boy in the next room, hearing them, laughed also.

"Well, how in the world did that Calico Clown come to be in my pocket?" exclaimed the man. He took the toy out, turned it over and looked at it from all sides. As he did so he happened to punch the Clown in the chest, and of course the Clown banged his cymbals together, as he had been taught to do in the workshop of Santa Claus, where he had been made.

And as the cymbals tinkled and clanged the typewriter girl laughed harder than ever. Then the man happened to pull one of the strings, and the Clown kicked up his legs. The office boy was looking into the room just then, and, seeing this antic of the jolly red and yellow chap, the office boy laughed out loud.

"Dear me! I'm glad every one in this office is so good-natured," thought the Clown to himself. "And I certainly am glad to get out of that Man's pocket. I was nearly smothered there, but of course it was better than being in the tree. I'll do some more tricks for them if the Man pulls more strings."

And the Man did. He pulled the strings fastened to the Clown's arms, and they jiggled and joggled in a merry fashion, so the girl and the office boy laughed harder than ever.

"Well, how in the world did that Clown toy come to be in my pocket?

That's what I want to know," said the Man, very much puzzled.

"Maybe one of the children put it in," suggested the girl. She knew the Man had children at home.

"No, I hardly think it was any of MY children," said the Man. "Arnold has no toy like this. He has a Bold Tin Soldier, as he calls him, and some soldier men. And my little girl, Mirabell, has a Lamb on Wheels. But neither of them has a Calico Clown."

"Perhaps some of their playmates called at your house, to have fun with Arnold or Mirabell," said the typewriter girl, "and they may have dropped the Clown into your pocket as your coat hung on the rack."

"Yes, that could have happened," said the Man. "But I remember I put my hand in my pocket as I left the house, to make sure I had some letters I was to mail. The Clown was not in my pocket then. He must have got in after I left my house. And how could that happen, I should like to know! I didn't go in any place. How could it have happened?"

Of course neither the office boy nor the typewriter girl could tell. They had not seen the Calico Clown fall from the tree into the pocket of the Man as he passed underneath. And even the Man himself had not seen this.

"It's very queer," said the father of Mirabell and Arnold. "The only way it could have happened that I can think of is that some children I passed on the street may have tossed the Clown into my pocket. I have very large ones in this coat, and sometimes they stand wide open."

The Calico Clown stayed in the office all that day. It was the first time he had ever been to business, and he rather liked it as a change. Very few toys ever have the chance he had. He sat up on the Man's desk and watched the girl click at the typewriter, and he watched the office boy come in and out. The office boy looked at the Clown, too.

"I'm going to have some fun with him when the Boss goes out to lunch," said the office boy to himself.

Now the Clown felt rather strange in the office. His part in life was to make joy and laughter, and he could not do it sitting up straight and stiff on a desk. He looked around, and he saw, not far from him, a jolly little man, like a dwarf.

"I wish I could speak to him," thought the Clown. "He looks as if he belonged to the toy family."

And you can imagine how surprised the Clown was when, all of a sudden, the Man lifted the head right off the queer-looking little dwarf and dipped his pen down inside him!

"Why, he's an ink well!" thought the Clown. "That's what he is! An ink well! And his head comes off the same as the Porcelain Cat's head lifts off for matches to be put inside her. How very odd! I'd like to talk to that chap."

When the Man went out to lunch, into the office hurried the office boy with a grin on his face.

"What do you want?" asked the typewriter girl. "I want to make that

Clown jiggle," was the answer. "I'm going to have some fun with him."

"No, you mustn't!" exclaimed the girl. "The Boss won't like it if you touch him. If you break him—"

"Aw, I won't break him!" cried the boy. "Let me have him!"

He made a grab for the Calico Clown, and the girl tried to stop the boy. As a result the Clown was knocked off the desk to the floor.

"Oh, dear! I hope my glued leg is not broken!" thought the Clown.

CHAPTER VII

IN THE WASH-BASKET

"There, now look what you did!" cried the girl.

"I didn't do it! You did!" said the boy. "If you hadn't jiggled it out of my hand when I was taking it down it wouldn't have fallen."

I don't know how long they might have gone on disputing in this fashion if the office boy from next door had not poked his head in and called:

"What's the matter?"

Then he saw the Calico Clown lying on the floor and he added:

"Has Santa Claus been here?" and he laughed.

"It came out of the pocket of the Boss," explained the first office boy. "He put it on his desk. I was going to look at it and pull the strings, 'cause the Boss is out to lunch, but she jiggled my hand and made me drop it. Now it's busted."

"Maybe it isn't," said the second office boy. "I'll see."

He picked the Calico Clown up off the floor, punched him in the chest, and the gay red and yellow chap banged his cymbals together.

"He's all right so far," said the second office boy. "Now we'll pull the strings."

"And there's where trouble may come in," thought the Calico Clown himself, for he heard and saw and felt all that went on. "I'm almost sure my glued leg is broken," said the Clown to himself.

But when the strings were pulled, one after another, and the arms and legs and head of the funny fellow twisted and turned and jerked, the two office boys and the typewriter girl laughed. And the Clown himself was glad, for he felt that he was not broken.

"If the Boss comes in and finds you playing with that Clown you'll catch it," said the girl to the first office boy, after a while.

"I guess I'd better put him back on the desk. I'm going out to get my dinner pretty soon," the boy said.

And a little later, while the girl was in an outer office looking over some papers and while the Man was still at his lunch and while the office boy was out getting something to eat, the Calico Clown was left alone with the Ink-Well Dwarf.

"How do you do?" politely asked the Clown.

[Illustration: Calico Clown Has a Chat With Ink-Well Dwarf.]

"Very well, thank you," answered the Dwarf. "And how are you? Where did you come from? Are you going to work here?"

"I never work!" exclaimed the Clown. "I am only to make jolly fun and laughter."

"Then this is no place for you," went on the Dwarf. "This is an office, and we must all work, though I must admit that those boys seem to get as much fun out of it as any one. They're always skylarking, cutting up, and playing jokes. But I work myself. I hold ink for the Boss."

"I see you do," answered the Clown. "I suppose I don't really belong here, made only for fun, as I am. And I did not want to come here. It was quite accidental. I was brought."

"How!" asked the Ink-Well Dwarf.

"In the pocket of the Man they call the Boss," was the reply. And then the Clown told of how he had fallen out of the tree.

All the remainder of the day the Calico Clown sat on the desk of the

Man, wondering what would happen to him. At last he found out.

At the close of the afternoon, when no more business was to be done, the Man arose and closed his desk. He put papers in his different pockets to take home with him, and then he saw the Calico Clown.

"Oh, I mustn't forget you!" he said, speaking out loud as he sometimes did when alone. And he was alone in the office now, for the boy and the typewriter girl had gone. "I'll take you home and ask Arnold or Mirabell to whom you belong," went on the man. "You are some child's toy, I'm sure of that, and one of my children may know where you live."

The Calico Clown knew this to be so, and he knew that either Arnold or

Mirabell would at once be able to say that the Clown belonged to

Sidney, for they had seen Sidney playing with this toy.

"Back into my pocket you go!" said the Man, and he took the Clown down off the top of the desk. "There are a lot of handkerchiefs in that pocket," the man went on. "They'll make a good, soft bed for you to lie on."

And, surely enough, there was a soft bed of handkerchiefs for the Calico Clown. They were handkerchiefs the man had been carrying in his pocket for some time, and he had forgotten to put them in the wash, as his wife, over and over again, had told him to do.

A little later, with the Calico Clown nestled down in among a pile of handkerchiefs in his pocket, the Man started for home from his office.

"Well, I am certainly doing some traveling this day," thought the Clown, as he reposed in the Man's pocket. "First I am carried up a tree, and then I fall down. Next I am taken to an office, just as if I were in business like the Ink-Well Dwarf, and now I am being taken to the home of Mirabell and Arnold. I wonder what will happen next."

He did not have to wait long to find out.

Down the street walked the Man, and soon he was within sight of his home, where Mirabell and Arnold lived. The two children were out in front, waiting for their father. As soon as they saw him coming they stopped swinging on the gate and cried:

"Here comes Daddy!"

He waved his hand to them.

Down the street they raced to meet him, and taking hold of his hands, one on either side, they led him toward the house.

Just then out of the side gate came Mandy, the jolly fat colored washer-woman. She had a basket full of clothes on a small express wagon.

"Oh, that reminds me!" exclaimed Mirabell's father. "I'll put these handkerchiefs from my pocket in your basket of wash, Mandy! You can take them home with you, wash them clean and iron them and bring them back to me."

"'Deed an' dat's just what I can do!" exclaimed Mandy, smiling broadly. "Put 'em right down yeah in mah basket!"

She turned back the sheet she had spread over the soiled clothes and made a little place down in one corner for the Man to put his handkerchiefs.

There was quite a bundle of them, all wadded together.

"There, you can tell Mother I didn't forget my handkerchiefs this time," said Daddy to his two children. "You saw me put them in the wash, didn't you?"

"Yes, Daddy, we did!" exclaimed Mirabell. "And, oh, you ought to see what happened to my Lamb on Wheels to-day!"

"What happened?" asked Daddy, as he straightened up after having stooped down to thrust the handkerchiefs into the basket.

"Why, Arnold's Bold Tin Soldier got caught in the curly wool on my Lamb's back," explained Mirabell, "and they both fell into the flour barrel!"

"That WAS funny!" laughed Daddy. And he was thinking so much about this and laughing so with Arnold and Mirabell that he never stopped to think of the Calico Clown in among the handkerchiefs he had put in the wash-basket.

But that is what he had done. He had thrust the Clown, with the handkerchiefs, down in Mandy's basket of soiled clothes.

"Oh, my! Oh, dear me! Oh, what is going to happen now?" thought the Calico Clown as he felt himself covered up and taken away. "Oh, if I could only tell Mirabell or Arnold I am here. Oh, this is dreadful."

But he could do nothing! Away he was taken in the wash-basket.

CHAPTER VIII

DOWN IN A DEEP HOLE

Daddy hurried into the house with Mirabell and Arnold. The children were eager to show their father into what a funny pickle the Bold Tin Soldier and the Lamb on Wheels had got. Of course, it wasn't exactly a "pickle." I only call it that for fun. It was really the flour barrel into which the two toys had fallen.

"How did it happen?" asked Daddy, as the children brought out their playthings, the Soldier still entangled in the Lamb's wool, and both of them white with flour.

"It happened when we were in the kitchen watching the cook make a cake," explained Mirabell. "I was playing with my Lamb on the floor and I lifted her up to let her see how nice the cake looked."

"But what about your Soldier, Arnold?" asked Daddy.

"Oh, I had set my Soldier Captain on the back of Mirabell's Lamb to give him a ride," explained the little boy.

"I said he could," remarked Mirabell.

"And when she lifted her Lamb up she lifted my Soldier up, too," added

Arnold.

"And then!" burst out Mirabell, laughing, "my foot slipped and I let go of my Lamb on Wheels, and she fell into the flour barrel, and so did Arnold's Bold Tin Soldier."

"And they were a sight, all white and covered with flour!" exclaimed the little boy.

But now we must see what happened to the Calico Clown.

At first he was very uncomfortable, stuck down in among the soiled clothes. He feared he would smother; but really he did not need much air, and he soon found he was getting all he needed. The clothes were so soft that they did not crush him, and—he was not near any of Mirabell's or Arnold's play clothes—he soon found that they were not badly soiled. So, after getting over his first distaste, he began rather to like the ride in the little express wagon.

"It isn't as smooth as an automobile," thought the Calico Clown, "but it is jolly for a change. The only thing that's worrying me is what is going to happen next; and to know whether or not I shall ever see Sidney again."

And at this time, which was early in the evening, Sidney was still looking everywhere for his Calico Clown. The little boy told his mother and sister how he and Herbert had left the Clown and the Monkey on a Stick on the porch while they went to get bread and jam.

"And when we came back my Monkey was there," said Herbert, "but Sid's

Clown was gone."

"It is very strange where your toy has got to," said Mother. She helped Sidney and Herbert look, but the Clown seemed gone forever, and Sidney felt sorry.

"Now we can never have that circus," he said to his brother.

"Oh, maybe he'll be found some day," was the answer. But Sidney sadly shook his head.

Trundling the little express wagon with her basket of clothes along the streets, Mandy finally reached her home where she did the washing and ironing. Her children were waiting for her to come to supper. Liza Ann, the oldest girl, had set the table, and Jim, the next oldest boy, was out on the steps watching for his mother, just as Arnold and Mirabell watched for their daddy.

"Is de table all set, honey?" asked Mandy of Liza Ann. "I hopes it is, 'cause I wants to put dese yeah clothes in to soak after I eats."

"De table is all sot," explained Liza Ann. "An' de meat an' taters is all ready to hotten up."

"Dass good," sighed Mandy, for she was rather tired. "I'll jest leave these yeah clothes till after supper," she went on, putting the basket down in a corner of the room.

"Dear me! I wonder how much longer I shall have to stay here," thought the Calico Clown, tucked away under the sheet and in the pile of handkerchiefs. "Aren't they ever going to let me out? This is worse than being in jail!"

But at last Mandy's supper was finished, and, with Liza Ann and Jim to help her sort the clothes, she filled a tub with water and began. The big sheet was taken off the top of the basket, and then Liza Ann reached in and took up the bundle of handkerchiefs.

"You wants to be keerful o' dem, honey," said her mother. "Dem's de bestest an' most special hankowitches o' Mirabell's pa, an' he's very 'tickler how dey is washed. Better let me have dem, honey."

Mandy reached over to take the handkerchiefs from Liza Ann, and at that moment the little colored girl saw something red and yellow among them.

"Oh, what a funny handkowitch!" she called, and the next moment they all saw the Calico Clown. Mandy took him out of the bundle.

"Oh, Mammy! I want him!" cried Jim.

"Nope! He's mine! I saw him, fustest!" exclaimed Liza Ann, and she reached for the Calico Clown.

"Wait a minute, now, chilluns. Wait a minute!" said Mandy, and she held the toy close to her breast. "Dish yeah don't belongs to us."

"But it come in de basket of wash, Mammy!" said Jim. "Why can't we keep it?"

"'Cause tain't belongin' to us," answered his mother. "I can jest guess how it come in. Mirabell or Arnold, dey done drop it in dere Daddy's pocket, an' he didn't know nothin' about its bein' in. He took it out wif his hankowitches, and put it in mah basket of wash. An' I brung it home. My! My! It suah is funny how it happened!"

She held the Calico Clown up and looked at him.

"Oh, ain't he jest grand!" cried Jim, his eyes shining with delight.

"He suah is a gay fellow all right," said Mandy.

Liza Ann reached up and pulled one of the Clown's strings. Quickly his legs jiggled and he cut some funny capers.

"Oh, my! Dat suah is scrumptious!" laughed the little colored girl.

"Oh, Mammy, jest let us play with him a little while!" begged Jim.

"Den I'll take him back to where he belongs."

"All right," agreed Mandy. "But be mighty keerful of him! If dat Calico Clown should get busted Mirabell or Arnold is gwine to feel mighty bad!"

You see she didn't know the Clown belonged to Sidney, and not to either Mirabell or Arnold.

"Come on, we'll have some fun wif him!" said Liza Ann to her brother.

And then, while their mother put the clothes to soak, the children played with the Calico Clown. They were good and gentle children, and the gay toy did not in the least mind clanging his cymbals for them or doing his funny dance. He jiggled and joggled his arms and legs, and went through such funny antics that Jim and Liza Ann laughed again and again.

"Po' li'l honey lambs!" said Mandy with a sigh, as she bent over the wash tub. "I wish dey had some toys of dere own. But den I'se got good clean and soft watah to wash wif, an' dat's a blessin'! Lots of folks hasn't got only hard watah, what won't make no suds."

After the clothes had been put to soak in a tub Mandy dried her hands and sat and looked at Liza Ann and Jim playing with the Calico Clown.

"Come now, you'd better get ready to take him back," she said to Jim, after a while.

"Does you mean to take him back where you got de basket of wash,

Mammy?" asked the colored boy.

"Yes," his mother answered. "You know de big green house. You's been dere befo', honey. You go dere now, Jim—tisn't late yet—an' you take back dis Clown. Tell Mirabell or Arnold dat it got in de wash wif dere daddy's pocket hankowitches."

"All right," said Jim, with a sigh. "I will. But I suah does wish we could keep him!"

"So do I," sighed Liza Ann in a low voice.

"Well, maybe some day I can make money enough to git you somethin' to play wif," said their mother.

As she had said, it was not late, though the sun had set. It was a warm, summer night, and the moon was shining brightly. Jim knew the way to the house where Mirabell and Arnold lived, for he had often gone there both with his mother and alone, either to get or bring back the clothes.

With the Calico Clown wrapped in a piece of paper, Jim set off on his trip. He hurried along, thinking how nice it would be if he had a toy like that. He was wondering how long it would be before his mother could earn enough money to buy one when, just as he turned into the yard of the house where Arnold and Mirabell lived, Jim stumbled and fell.

The Calico Clown shot out of his hands, and the poor toy, as he flew along, thought to himself:

"Oh, what is happening now!"

The next moment he fell into a deep hole, and only that he grasped the long grass at the edge of it, Jim would have fallen in himself.

"Fo' de lan' sakes!" exclaimed the little colored boy as he picked himself up. "What have done gone an' happened now?"

CHAPTER IX

BACK HOME

The door of the house in which Arnold and Mirabell lived opened, and their daddy looked out toward the front yard. He had heard the grunt made by Jim when the little colored boy fell down and dropped the Calico Clown into a hole.

"Is anybody there?" asked Mirabell's father.

"I'se heah!" exclaimed Jim, as he slowly arose. "I was bringin' back de Calico Clown, an' I 'mos' fell into a big hole."

"There, Father! I told you that hole ought to be covered up!" exclaimed Mirabell's mother, who had also come to the door.

"Oh, no'm! I didn't fall in!" answered Jim, who heard what was said. "But I almos' did, an' I guess de Clown he fell in complete an' altogether."

"The Clown? What do you mean?" asked Daddy.

"De Clown what got in Mammy's basket of wash," explained the little colored boy.

By this time he had picked himself up, and in the light that streamed out from the open door of the house he saw the hole into which he had so nearly fallen. It was a hole dug by a man who had come to fix the sewer pipes that day, and when night came he had not finished. He left a deep, wide, gaping hole just beside the front walk.

Arnold, Mirabell and the others in the house knew of the hole, and kept away from it. In the daylight, when Mandy had taken away the wash, she had seen it and had not fallen in. But poor Jim, coming after dark, had stumbled in the thick grass and had nearly plumped himself in.

As for the Clown—well, there he was down in the dirt at the bottom of the hole!

"I wonder what is the matter with me!" thought the gay red and yellow fellow as he came to a stop in some soft dirt. "I seem to be very unlucky!"

"What does Jim mean about a Clown falling in the hole?" asked Arnold curiously.

"And a Clown being in the basket with the wash?" added Mirabell.

"I think I can tell you," their father answered, suddenly remembering what he had put in his pocket to bring home from the office. "But first I will put some boards over the hole the plumber left so no one else will fall in, or nearly fall in."

"You'll get the Clown up, won't you, Daddy?" asked Mirabell. "Maybe it's like the one Sidney had."

"Did Sidney have a Calico Clown with one leg red and the other leg yellow?" asked Daddy.

"Yes, and it did all sorts of funny tricks when you pulled the strings; and he clapped his cymbals when you punched him in the chest," said Arnold.

"Well, then this must be Sidney's Clown. But how it came in my pocket is more than I can guess," said Daddy. "Yes, I'll get the Clown up out of the hole, and then I'll put some boards over it."

A lantern was brought out and flashed down into the hole. There, on the bottom, lay the Calico Clown.

"I'll bring him up!" offered Jim, and quickly he climbed down, caught hold of the gay toy, and climbed out again.

"Thank you, Jim," said Daddy.

"Yes, that's Sidney's Clown," declared Arnold, when he had looked at the red and yellow chap. "But how did he get in the basket of clothes?"

"That's quite a long story," said Daddy. "Come into the house and I'll tell you. Did your mother send you back with the Clown, Jim?" he asked of the little colored boy.

"Yes'm—I mean yes, sah!" Jim answered. "He was in de basket all done wrapped up in hankowitches."

"Those were the handkerchiefs I took from my pocket and put in Mandy's basket when I met her at the gate," said Mirabell's daddy. "And so you found him, Jim!"

"Yes'm—I mean yes, sah! Me an' Liza Ann found him. He's a jolly good Clown; but Mammy, she wouldn't let us keep him 'cause as how she said he belonged to Mirabell or Arnold."

"No, he doesn't live here," said Arnold. "Oh, Sid will be so glad to get him back!"

"I suppose you and your sister felt bad about losing the Clown," said

Daddy to Jim. "Didn't you?"

"I suahly did!" exclaimed the little colored boy. "So did Liza Ann."

Daddy and Mother talked softly together a moment, and then Mother hurried away to come back with something that made Jim's eyes sparkle and open wide.

For she had a little toy engine, which could be wound up with a key and sent whizzing along. And there was a fine Jumping Jack, which jiggled almost as nicely as did the Calico Clown.

"Here are two toys that Arnold and Mirabell are through with," said

Mother, with a smile at Jim. "They are not broken, and they will each

go. Perhaps you will like them almost as much as you did the Calico

Clown."

"Oh, golly!" cried Jim. "We'll like 'em better! 'Cause dere's two of 'em—one fo' each of us! Oh, we's eber so much obligedness."

Clasping the two toys in his little brown hands, away Jim raced in the darkness to tell his sister the good news. The Jumping Jack was for her and the toy engine for him. And I may as well tell you now that the two children were made perfectly happy with their toys—just as happy as they would have been with the Calico Clown.

"Well, thank goodness, I think my adventures are over for the night," thought the Clown, as he was taken into Mirabell's house and the dirt brushed off his red and yellow trousers. "This has been such a day! Oh, SUCH a day!"

And indeed it had been from the time he fell out of the tree into the Man's coat pocket until Jim stumbled with him and he fell into the hole.

"Sidney will be glad to get his Clown back," went on Arnold, when the toy had been set on the table where Daddy took his place to tell the evening story.

"I wish we could take it to him now," said Mirabell.

"Mayn't we?" asked her brother.

"It is getting late," said their mother. "You may take the toy over the first thing in the morning."

"But all the while Sidney will be wondering where his Clown is," objected the little girl.

"I know what we can do!" exclaimed Arnold. "We can telephone and tell him it's here."

"Yes, we can do that," said Daddy.

So, a little later, Sidney was told, over the telephone, that his lost Calico Clown had been found. The story was briefly told of how it had got into the wash-basket after having been found in Daddy's pocket and taken to the office.

"Oh, I'm so glad!" cried Sidney. "I'll be over the first thing in the morning to get him."

"But what I'm wondering about is how the Clown got in my pocket," said Daddy, with a puzzled look on his face. "If you children didn't put it there, who did?" and he looked at Mirabell and Arnold.

And I might say that this was always a mystery, as much so as the

Clown's riddle about what made more noise than a pig under a gate.

Daddy told Mirabell and Arnold their usual good-night story. Then the children went to bed and Mother put the Calico Clown on the mantelpiece where he would be safe for the night.

"Whoever sees Sidney first in the morning," said Mother, as she, too, got ready to go to bed, "may be the one to give him his toy."

Then the lights were put out and the house was still and quiet. Ordinarily, when this time came, the Calico Clown, like the other toys, would have been at his liveliest. But now he was so tired, with all his adventures of the day, that he just gave a long sigh and said:

"I am not going to stir! I am just going to lie down here and sleep until morning! Enough has happened for one day."

So he stretched out, with a pen wiper for a cushion, and went to sleep.

Bright and early the next morning Sidney ran over to the house of his cousins.

"Is my Calico Clown here?" he cried.

"Yes," answered Arnold, who was also up. "I'll get him for you."

"Oh, thank you!" said Sidney, when he had his toy once more. And a little later the Calico Clown was back home. But his adventures were not over.

CHAPTER X

THE TOY PARTY

"Oh, Sidney! aren't you glad you have your Calico Clown back?" cried his sister Madeline when she saw her brother coming toward the house with his toy which he had got at Arnold's home. "I just guess I am!" said the little boy. "I thought I'd never see him again."

"And I'm glad, too," cried Herbert, as he made his Monkey go up and down the Stick. "Now we can get ready for our circus."

"Are you going to have a show?" asked Madeline.

"Yes," answered Sidney. "We have a Clown and a Monkey, and they're always the funniest things in a circus. Don't you remember when we had the show with my Monkey in it?"

"Yes. And that was lots of fun," said Madeline. "But I know something better than a show."

"What?" Sidney asked.

"A party," went on Madeline. "Let's have a Toy Party. That will be better than a show, even a circus show."

Sidney wanted to know how it would be better, and Madeline said:

"'Cause you can have things to eat at a Toy Party, and you can't always have things at a circus, lessen you buy 'em; and maybe not then, 'cepting peanuts and lemonade. Let's have a Toy Party and we can get mother to give us real things to eat."

"Oh, that will be fun!" cried Sidney. "I should say so!" agreed

Herbert.

"And we'll ask Dorothy to bring her Sawdust Doll," said Madeline,

"Arnold can bring his Bold Tin Soldier, and Mirabell her Lamb on

Wheels. And I'll bring my Candy Rabbit."

"You did have a party for him," said Herbert.

"Well, this one can be for Sid's Calico Clown," explained Madeline.

"And you can bring your Monkey on a Stick, Herb."

The idea of a Toy Party seemed to please the two boys, and Madeline was glad she had thought of it. She lost no time in getting ready for it.

"I'll go and put a new ribbon on the neck of my Candy Rabbit," she said to her brothers. "You get your Monkey and Clown all nice and clean, and then I'll ask Mother if Cook can make a special cake."

"My Monkey is clean enough," said Herbert. "Dirt doesn't show on him, anyhow. He's colored brown."

"And my Clown's pretty good, even if he did fall in a dirt hole," went on Sidney. "A Clown has to be a little dirty, for he falls all over the circus ring, you know."

"There isn't going to be any circus ring at our Toy Party," laughed

Madeline. "Now I'll go and see about the cake."

"And we'll go and tell Dick, Arnold and the girls," said Sidney. "Here, Madeline, please keep my Calico Clown for me until I come back."

Away he ran with his brother, who carried the Monkey on a Stick. The Calico Clown rather hoped the long-tailed chap would be left to keep him company, but it was not to be just yet.

"But perhaps I can talk to the Candy Rabbit while Madeline is getting ready for the party," thought the Clown. "He and I are old friends."

But even this was not to be. Madeline probably did not think that the Clown would have liked to be with some of the other toys for a while. She just kept hold of the gay red and yellow fellow after her brother had handed him to her, and took him with her to the kitchen, where she knew her mother was.

"Oh, Mother! may Cook bake us a cake for the Toy Party?" cried

Madeline, and, not thinking what she was doing, she laid the Calico

Clown down in a large basket of oranges which the fruit man had just

set on the kitchen table.

"A cake for a Toy Party?" repeated Mother. "Yes, I think so. Tell me more about it."

So Madeline told about the Toy Party that was going to be held, and how the Sawdust Doll, the White Rocking Horse, and all the other jolly creatures were to come.

"Course they won't EAT the cake—only make believe," explained

Madeline. "We'll eat the cake—we children."

"Yes, I supposed you would," said Mother, with a laugh as she looked at Cook.

"And, please, may I help?" asked Madeline.

"Yes," promised Cook, and then, not thinking what she was doing and not seeing the Calico Clown, who had slipped away down in among the oranges, she took the basket of fruit from the table.

"I'll just set the oranges in the ice box," she said. "They need to be well chilled for the orangeade, and it's a hot day."

And that is how it was that the Clown, a little later, found himself beginning to feel freezing cold. He had not minded being laid for a time in with the golden, yellow fruit. It smelled so nice that he shut his eyes and breathed deep of the perfume. He even took a little sleep. And then, the next thing he knew, he felt a breath of cold air after a door was slammed shut.

"Dear me! what can have happened now?" said the Calico Clown, suddenly awakening. "Am I back again at the North Pole workshop of Santa Claus? It feels like it, but it doesn't look like it. For his shop was nice and light, though it was sometimes cold. Here it is dark."

"Well, I simply am freezing!" went on the Clown. "I've got to keep warm, somehow!"

So what did he do but stand up and begin to dance around among the oranges. Up and down, first to this side and then to the other danced the jolly fellow, jerking his arms and swinging his legs. He clapped his hands together to warm them, and his cymbals clanged in the cold, frosty air of the ice box.

After a while the Clown began to feel warmer. But as soon as he stopped jumping around he felt cold again.

"I've got to keep moving, that's all there is to it!" he said to himself, and he had to dance again.

Really he must have looked funny, doing a jig on a basket of oranges, but it was not so funny for the poor Clown himself. He was beginning to get tired, and he was wondering how long he would have to keep up his exercise, when the ice-box door suddenly opened and Cook lifted out a bowl of cream.

"Oh, for the love of trading stamps!" she cried, as she saw the Clown in among the oranges. "How did you ever get there? You must be almost frozen!"

And the poor fellow would have been, if he had not danced.

"I certainly didn't see you there when I put the fruit in the ice box," went on the cook. "Madeline must have put you among the oranges."

And, of course, this was just what had happened. Naturally you may say that the reason the cook saw the Clown the second time, after she opened the ice-box door, was because some of the oranges rolled to one side, allowing the Clown to be seen. But that isn't how it happened at all. The Clown simply climbed out from among the fruit to dance and keep himself warm, and that's how he happened to be seen.

"Oh, dear me! To think I should do a thing like that!" cried Madeline, when the cook handed her the Calico Clown. "Sidney might have thought his toy was lost again if you hadn't found him. Now we'll bake the cake, and I'll put the Clown by the stove to get warm."

After a while everything was ready for the party. The cake was baked and covered with icing. There were also some crullers and some cookies.

Herbert, Sidney and Mirabell put on their party clothes, and with the Monkey on a Stick nicely brushed, the Candy Rabbit with a new ribbon on his neck, and with the last specks of dirt shaken off the red and yellow trousers of the Clown, they all waited for the others to come.

"Here's Dorothy with her Sawdust Doll!" cried Madeline, running to the window.

[Illustration with caption: "Oh, I Have So Many Things to Tell You!"]

"Yes, and Arnold is helping Dick carry over the White Rocking Horse," added Sidney. "Oh, what fun we'll have!"

"I hope Arnold brought his Bold Tin Soldier Captain and all the others," said Herbert.

Arnold brought them, and his sister Mirabell came with her Lamb on

Wheels.

Then such fun as there was at the Toy Party! I really don't know whether the children or the toys enjoyed it most. But I do know that the children ate the cakes and cookies, which was something the toys could not do.

While Dick, Dorothy and the other boys and girls were in the room, the toys could not speak to one another. But when, in playing some game the lads and lassies went out into the yard, the toys had their chance.

"Oh, I have so many things to tell you!" said the Calico Clown. "I have had so many adventures!"

Then he related how the monkey had taken him up into the tree and how finally he had got back home.

"Quite remarkable," said the Lamb on Wheels. "You certainly have—

Ouch! Oh, dear!" said the Lamb, suddenly switching one of her legs.

"What's the matter?" asked the Bold Tin Soldier. "If anybody is teasing you I'll make him stop!" and he drew his sword and looked very fierce—as all tin soldiers look.

"It was nothing," said the Lamb on Wheels. "Just a pang of rheumatism. The remains of the cold I caught in one of my wheels the time I made the voyage down the brook on the raft the boys built."

Then the Sawdust Doll told of a little adventure she had had recently, when she was left in the wrong doll carriage by mistake and was taken home to the wrong house.

"Nothing as remarkable as jumping downstairs and scaring the burglars has happened to me," said the White Rocking Horse. "But Dick was riding me in the kitchen the other day and he ran me over an egg."

"Did it hurt you?" asked the Monkey.

"No; but it spoiled the egg," said the Horse, laughing.

"Well, I must say it is very nice of the children to get up a party for us like this," said the Calico Clown. "And I, for one—"

"Hush! Here they come! We must be very still and quiet!" whispered the

Candy Rabbit.

And back into the room trooped the merry children, and they played more games and ate more cake until none was left, and then the party was over.

"Well, I certainly have come to a happy home," thought the Calico

Clown, when he was put to bed that night on a closet shelf. "This is

just as jolly as being in the store!" And he snuggled up close to the

Candy Rabbit and the Monkey on a Stick. Then they all went to sleep.

THE END